Murphy's Three Homes

To Eli, Theo, and the real dog, Murphy — JLG

To Basil, Watson, and Ripley, my pups. You taught me patience, the ability to love unconditionally, and how to find joy in the little things — KO

Published by
MAGINATION PRESS
An Educational Publishing Foundation Book
American Psychological Association
750 First Street, NE
Washington, DC 20002

For more information about our books, including a complete catalog, please write to us, call 1-800-374-2721, or visit our website at www.maginationpress.com.

Art Director: Susan K. White
Printed by Worzalla, Stevens Point, Wisconsin

Library of Congress Cataloging-in-Publication Data

Gilman, Jan Levinson.
Murphy's three homes : a story for children in foster care / by Jan Levinson Gilman ; illustrated by Kathy O'Malley.
p. cm.
Summary: A puppy describes the emotional ups and downs of being in multiple foster homes and living in unfamiliar surroundings. Includes note to parents.
ISBN-13: 978-1-4338-0384-0 (hardcover : alk. paper)
ISBN-10: 1-4338-0384-4 (hardcover : alk. paper)
ISBN-13: 978-1-4338-0385-7 (pbk. : alk. paper)
ISBN-10: 1-4338-0385-2 (pbk. : alk. paper) [1. Foster home care—Fiction. 2. Dogs—Fiction.]
I. O'Malley, Kathy, ill. II. Title.
PZ7.G43323Mu 2008
[E]—dc22   2008017587

10 9 8 7 6 5 4 3 2 1

Murphy's Three Homes

a story for children in foster care

by Jan Levinson Gilman
illustrated by Kathy O'Malley

MAGINATION PRESS WASHINGTON DC

American Psychological Association

My name is Murphy. I'm a Tibetan Terrier. We're little dogs that are supposed to bring our families good luck.

I have floppy ears and a long tail I curl up and wag back and forth when I'm happy. When I am sad or scared, my tail gets very droopy.

I love to play, even with things that might get me in trouble – like socks and stuff from the wastebasket.

People tell me I'm no different than any other Tibetan Terrier, but somehow I must be different because I've had three homes.

For a long time I thought it was my fault. I thought "maybe I'm a bad luck dog" instead of a good luck dog.

You see, my mom was pretty old when I was born. My two brothers and three sisters were too much for her to care for. My owners decided it would help my mom get strong again by finding us a new home.

That's how I wound up in my first home. It was a huge house filled with people and animals.

There was a Mom, Dad, and three different size kids. There were two big dogs and another animal I had never seen before. I learned it was a cat.

I tried to play with everyone that lived there, but everybody else seemed very busy in that big house. I couldn't figure it all out because everything was still so new. The other dogs knew where to eat, where to sleep, and where to go to the bathroom.

I'd always be the last to the food bowl, and there would only be a little left.

I was so hungry that I ate the cat food. The cat hissed at me, and the humans said, "No Murphy! That's not your food." (Anyway, it tasted pretty bad. Yuck!)

The family got mad at me whenever I had an accident in the house.

I was supposed to sit by the door and wait for them to take me outside.

Once, I got lost in that big house and I couldn't even find the door.

Everyone looked at me like I should have known my way around the house.

Sometimes I would play so hard that I would forget I had to go until it was too late.

One day I was sitting by the fence when the mailman came by. I was so happy to see him I thought I'd wag my tail right off! But he didn't pet me like the neighbors did. He just looked at me with a sad face and said, "Poor puppy."

The next day a truck with cages on the back stopped by my house. A man got out and knocked on our front door. I heard him say, "That puppy's undernourished. I'm taking him."

What did undernourished mean? I guessed it meant that I had been bad. I didn't understand that the nice mailman was worried about me because I wasn't getting enough to eat. The man in the truck took me to the animal shelter where there were lots of dogs and cats waiting for new homes.

The humans at the animal shelter took good care of me and gave me plenty of tasty food and a soft blanket to snuggle. I should have been happy to be safe, but I was confused and scared. I worried, "How long will I be here? Where is my mom? Where is my family?"

It seemed like a very long time until a new family picked me out and took me home.

They weren't like the first family. The man smiled and scratched my head and looked happy to have a new puppy. I was excited too. Would this be my home?

There were no kids or animals in this house. I even got my own bed, a squeaky toy to play with, and my very own food bowl. The man smiled and said, "Good boy, Murphy," when I went to the bathroom in the right place.

Things seemed almost perfect in my new home. But the man's wife didn't like when I was frisky in the house or when I jumped up when I wanted to play. She'd say, "Murphy, get down!" I tried to listen but sometimes I forgot.

One day I heard the man and lady arguing. I didn't mean to listen, but I knew it was about me. I heard her say, "Murphy can't stay here any more. He's scratching my legs with his puppy claws."

The man said, "He's just a puppy. He'll learn. I'll teach him."

"He won't learn fast enough He has to go!"

My tail drooped, but I kept my feelings inside.

But then the man said, "Just give him one more chance. I will remind him not to jump up on you."

"OK, just one more try."

I wanted to be happy that they were giving me one more chance. I liked the man and I sort of liked the lady too. She laughed when I chased my tail. But I was all mixed up. Could I really be good enough to stay? I hoped I could but a little voice inside me said, "Murphy, you're a bad luck dog."

I didn't jump for the next few days. The man kept saying, "Good Murphy. You're behaving so well."

But I wasn't good enough. One day,
when the man opened the door,
I leaped up on our neighbor. I looked
around and saw my owners
watching me. The man looked sad,
and the lady was shaking her head.

My heart sunk. I had lost my last chance. I knew I would have to leave, but I
didn't want to show them that it made me sad. I didn't want to say I was sorry.
I curled my tail up high and walked away to make them think I didn't care.
What difference would it make anyway? Inside I knew I was a bad luck dog.

Soon after that day another man and lady came to visit. They said, "Ohh" and "Aww! This is just the right kind of puppy for us." So they took me to their house.

It had a humongous yard filled with birds and a big pond that I could wade in. They introduced me to their cat, Magic, who liked playing with me.

I liked it so much at my new home, but deep down I was sure it wouldn't work. After all, I was a bad luck dog. I tried to be good. I ate my own food and not Magic's. I never went to the bathroom in the house. I tried not to jump up on people. Then I learned that the lady and the man didn't care if I jumped on them. They just laughed and wrestled with me.

Still, I felt sure something bad would happen.

And then one night something happened.

I was left in the bathroom. The doorbell kept ringing
and I heard lots of new voices in the house.
They were laughing and there was music playing.

Were they looking for another family to take me? I felt so alone and sad and angry. I began to pace up and down. That's when I saw it—a shiny wastebasket that was filled with trash. I knew I shouldn't get into it, but why not? They were probably giving me away again anyway. Why should I care? Why should I follow the rules?

I pushed over the wastebasket. And boy was it cool!
There was some tissue to chew on and a candy wrapper.
Yum! Humans get good food. Then there was a tube of
something green. I bit into it and it squirted out.
It was fun when the green stuff got all over the floor.

Something told me to stop. I just didn't listen.

Suddenly I heard footsteps. They got louder and louder. "Uh, oh," I thought, "Now I'm busted." My new owners walked into the room. They said, "C'mon Murphy. Let's show you off to our friends."

When they saw the trash all over the floor, the lady said, "Look what Murphy's done." The man shook his finger at me and said, "Bad dog!"

I didn't want them to send me away so I ran past them and out of the house. I had never been out alone in the dark before. I ran up the street and soon I was lost. But who cared? Who would look for me? On the outside I was just like every other Tibetan Terrier, but on the inside I was a bad luck dog.

It seemed like hours that I walked from yard to yard. I heard humans laughing and other dogs barking. Those dogs had a home. They must be good luck dogs.

In the distance I heard someone calling, "Murphy! Murphy, where are you?" It was the lady calling! "Come Murphy. Please come home."

Suddenly, the lady picked me up. Instead of being mad at me, the lady seemed so excited to see me. She hugged me tightly and said, "I was so worried about you. We were afraid we'd lost you for good. I'm so glad I found you."

She gave me such a big hug that I almost couldn't breathe, but I didn't care about breathing just then. I thought, "Even though I was naughty she left her party to look for me and she's really happy to find me."

The lady carried me all the way back to the house. I felt like it was my home too.

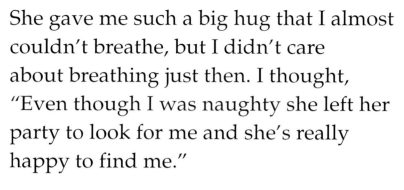

That night when I snuggled in my doggie bed, I wished that all dogs who believe they are bad luck dogs would discover that it isn't their fault…that they too can become good luck dogs.

29

Note to Caregivers and Other Adults

by Jan Levinson Gilman, PhD

Murphy is an adorable puppy experiencing some hard times in life. After being turned out of two different homes and a shelter, Murphy starts feeling like a "bad luck dog"—a dog that no one wants. Eventually, he is placed with a loving family, and begins feel happy, comfortable, and secure in his new home. Ultimately he learns that he is a good luck dog, just like all other Tibetan Terriers. Murphy's experiences are similar to those of many foster (or foster-adopt) children. Helping a child build and maintain positive self-esteem in the face of the adversity experienced by most foster children is the central theme of the book. By reading this book, your child may also find comfort in discovering he is not alone.

A Tool for Conversation

Murphy's Three Homes is meant to be read by a child and an adult together, although over time, children may want to re-read it on their own. The story mirrors the experience of many children who have been in foster homes. Murphy, as the quintessential foster child, can be used as a tool to acknowledge the children's experiences. The book aims to validate their feelings, to support their coping with uncertainty, to diminish their sense of isolation or aloneness, to decrease their confusion, to lighten any burdens of guilt or fault, to provide opportunities for them to speak about their experiences, and to offer—without false promises—messages that might sustain them.

As you read this book with your foster child:

- Convey to her that you are willing to listen. Children may tell their own stories about their past, their own feelings, and their own reactions.
- Let him know that he may have had experiences that are not mentioned in this book. This may help him feel more comfortable talking about his experiences, which in turn will help ease his adjustment to your home.
- Realize that many children may be reluctant to speak about their previous placements whereas others may only want to speak about one experience that the book has touched upon.

- Keep in mind that some children may not want to talk about the story at all when they first read it. They may save their thoughts and questions until such time as before bedtime or around a scheduled parental visit.
- Respond in an age-appropriate manner. For example, if a very young child asks, "What is the animal shelter?" you might respond that it is a place to keep animals safe until they find another home. With an older child, you might also explain how the animal shelter protects animals from abusive situations.
- If your foster child is seeing a therapist, you might find it helpful to inform the therapist that you are reading this book with her.
- If your foster child is willing to discuss issues raised in the book, you may want to ask open ended questions, such as "Why do you think Murphy believed he was a bad luck dog?" You might be able to guide the conversation from general to more specific questions like "What is Murphy feeling?" to "What do you think a kid would feel?" to "Have you ever felt this way?"

Identification of Feelings and Beliefs

Often adult caregivers can misunderstand or misinterpret a child's expression of emotions. With practice you can learn to interpret and respond to your child's emotions. Some of the many ways children express emotion are:

- Unexplained irritability;
- Unusual desire for attention and/or clingingness;
- Sudden bursts of energy;
- Withdrawal;
- Regression, such as having a toileting accident;
- Anger and aggressive behavior towards others.

If your child's behavior leads you to suspect that he has emotions he doesn't know how to express, you might want to try the following:

- Help him understand and identify his feelings. You might say, "I bet you feel left out sometimes when

I have to spend so much time taking care of your brother. Sometimes when people feel left out they really are jealous and angry." Giving a word to an emotion may help him clarify what he is feeling and make it easier for him to identify it another time.

- Find a time to gently encourage him to talk about what is bothering him. If you have some idea as to the cause, tentatively offer suggestions such as, "It seems like something is bothering you. I'm wondering if that phone call from your mother has upset you."
- Be prepared to listen non-judgmentally to your child's feelings. You might even say something as simple as, "I didn't know you felt that way. It's important for me to know how you're feeling."
- Avoid denying or minimizing his reality when he's expressing a feeling. His perception may be inaccurate, but the feelings are real, just the same. For example, "I understand that you feel mad when you get all the hand-me-downs and leftover clothes. I am proud of you for telling me how you feel."
- Let your child know that certain angry behaviors are unacceptable and offer an alternative solution to expressing what is frustrating or angering him. You might say, "You have every right to be angry. Let's figure out a way to express your mad feelings with words."
- Know that the desire to fix problems and find practical solutions can sometimes get in the way of discussing feelings. Talking through problems and identifying emotions can itself be beneficial to your child. For example, you might say, "Even grown-ups can have trouble fixing problems. Although it can't always fix things, sometimes it helps to just talk about how you are feeling and what is troubling you."

Listening to and acknowledging feelings takes time and patience, but it can create memorable childhood experiences and is an excellent way to establish trust with your child. For a foster child, it may be the first time his sentiments have been validated. The experience of empathy is essential to establishing his trust in the world. Just the simple act of listening and confirming an emotional experience may make the world seem like a safer place for your child.

Foster children experience a range of emotions and perceptions, and your foster child will experience some, if not all, of these:

Guilt. One of the most common issues among children in foster care is self-blame. If a placement failure occurs, she may start to believe that she caused it rather than understanding the greater scope of the issues that are involved. The child often believes that there is something wrong or defective about her that caused the problem. If your foster child expresses self-blame, provide an age-appropriate explanation of the cause(s) of the problem to show her she is not to blame, keeping in mind not to minimize her feelings. If your child does have a role in the failure, clearly delineate what is hers.

Confusion. A child in foster care is often confused when she is separated from her parents or siblings. She may have been given a simplistic answer, one that as she grows older does not fully explain the situation. Many young foster children struggle with this and will have questions about their early childhood and family history. Conferring with the child's social worker to learn more about her early history may provide answers to simple questions. Developing a timeline with a child helps put a complicated life course into perspective.

Your child may also feel confused about her new home — if the house is big, she may feel lost. She may wonder, "What are the family rules? What is the routine? Who is related to whom?" Your family's history may have very little meaning to her and conversations can be misunderstood. Just like any newcomer to an existing group, relationships and rules should be explained to a new child in the home and patiently repeated so that she can remember.

Grief and Loss. Children in foster care experience tremendous loss that is compounded each time they must leave a home for a new placement. Loss is expressed in sadness, hopelessness, behavioral regression, and anger. Your foster child may grieve the loss of possessions, people, and places, even if foster care provides relief or a reprieve from abuse. Children who are removed from their biological home may have lost everything familiar to them. Acknowledging loss and expressing empathy is essential. Loss resolution takes time, so have patience with your child as she copes with her losses. Remember that it is not unusual for a child who has lived in an abusive home to have some attachment to it despite the abuse. Even the most painful experience may have some positive value for your child.

Shame. Children may feel a sense of shame about the simple fact of being in foster care. Your child may express this shame in arrogance, disdain, or anger. Some children are more adept than others at hiding their shame by appearing nonchalant about an experience or by vociferously blaming others. Either of these tactics may be a defense against shame.

Anger. A child may be angry at her parents, social workers, or other adults whom she sees as responsible for her placement. She may be angry at decisions that are out of her control or with the abruptness of change in her life. She may be angry about expectations she feels she cannot meet.

Distrust. Life experiences often teach foster children to be distrustful. Many foster children test their families by acting out. Make it clear by your words and actions that the logical consequences for unacceptable behavior never include emotional rejection and exclusion. If there is a risk of expulsion from the home, let your child know the limits to which her behavior will be tolerated.

Loneliness. Foster children have difficulty sustaining primary relationships. A sense of belonging takes time to develop, so foster children often feel separate from those around them. This creates feelings of being alone and lonely. To help your child, spend time with him and give him lots of attention when he is new to the home. Make sure there everyone else in the household does so, as well. Explore his talents and interests and incorporate them into the family experience. For example, if he is fascinated by nature, take a family hike. If he likes Chinese food, make a family meal of Chinese food.

Additionally, provide common childhood experiences by helping your child connect to other children of similar age and development. Remember most foster children face more than their share of adversity, but that doesn't prevent them from being kids and having fun despite the turmoil in their world.

There Is Always Hope

An experience of unconditional acceptance provides foster children with a new basis for hope and ultimately trust. It is a fragile feeling that, with nurturing, will grow. As it grows, so does his self esteem and belief system. At his core, he is no longer an unacceptable, lonely, confused, or abandoned child, but like Murphy, he is a child who has lived with adversity but fundamentally is just like everyone else…he has just had multiple homes.

About the Author

DR. JAN GILMAN has a B.A. from U.C. Berkeley and a Ph.D. from the Wright Institute in Berkeley, California. She is a Clinical Psychologist living in Santa Rosa, California and has spent thirty years working with children and families. She combines her experience working with the adoption and foster care community with her lifelong love of animals in writing this metaphorical story about her real dog, Murphy. Dr. Gilman is married. She has two grown children and two grandchildren.

About the Illustrator

KATHY O'MALLEY knew she wanted to be an artist from the age of six. She graduated from Chicago's Columbia College, and has illustrated more than 40 children's books. Kathy works from her home studio overlooking her perennial gardens, watched by two loyal art critics, her fun-loving standard poodles.